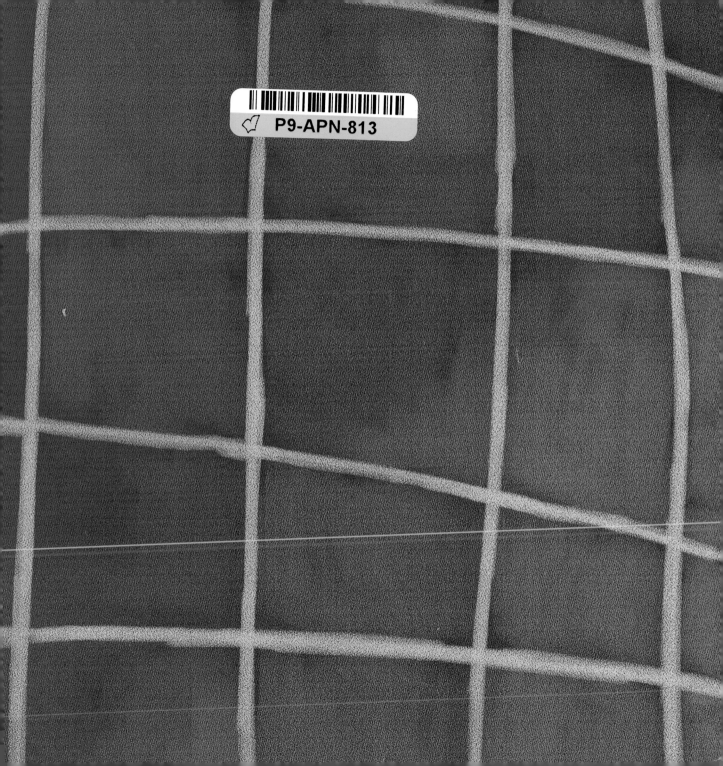

Published by Top That! Publishing plc
Tide Mill Way, Woodbridge, Suffolk, IP12 1AP, UK
www.topthatpublishing.com
Copyright © Top That! Publishing plc 2011
All rights reserved
0 2 4 6 8 9 7 5 3 1
Printed and bound in China

Creative Director—Simon Couchman
Editorial Director—Daniel Graham

Written by Gordon Volke
Illustrated by Alexia Orkrania

ISBN 978-1-84956-878-4

Printed and bound in China

Hullabaloo!

Written by Gordon Volke

There's a donkey called Drew
Making a *hullabaloo* at the zoo.

There's a cockatoo who squawks out "Boo!"
And a donkey called Drew
Making a *hullabaloo* at the zoo.

The chimp twins, Daisy and Maisie,
enjoy their tea-for-two,
With the cockatoo who squawks out "Boo!"
And a donkey called Drew

Making a *hullabaloo* at the zoo.

There are hopping bunnies with lots of grass to chew,
While the chimp twins, Daisy and Maisie,
enjoy their tea-for-two,
With the cockatoo who squawks out "Boo!"
And a donkey called Drew

Making a *hullabaloo* at the zoo.

There's a calf called Cassie who keeps on saying "Moo!"
And hopping bunnies with lots of grass to chew,
While the chimp twins, Daisy and Maisie,
enjoy their tea-for-two,
With the cockatoo who squawks out "Boo!"
And a donkey called Drew

Making a *hullabaloo*
at the zoo.

There are downy ducklings marching through!
Past a calf called Cassie who keeps on saying "Moo!"
And hopping bunnies with lots of grass to chew,
While the chimp twins, Daisy and Maisie,
enjoy their tea-for-two,
With the cockatoo who squawks out "Boo!"
And a donkey called Drew

Making a *hullabaloo* at the zoo.

There's a roo called Sue with her joey, Blue,
who bounce around (that's all they do!)
And downy ducklings marching through!
Past a calf called Cassie who keeps on saying "Moo!"
And hopping bunnies with lots of grass to chew,

While the chimp twins, Daisy and Maisie, enjoy their tea-for-two,
With the cockatoo who squawks out "Boo!"
And a donkey called Drew
Making a *hullabaloo* at the zoo.

There are baby owls who sit and say "Twit-to-woo!"
Beside a roo called Sue with her joey, Blue,
who bounce around (that's all they do!)
And downy ducklings marching through!
Past a calf called Cassie who keeps on saying "Moo!"
And hopping bunnies with lots of grass to chew,
While the chimp twins, Daisy and Maisie, enjoy their tea-for-two,
With the cockatoo who squawks out "Boo!"
And a donkey called Drew

Making a *hullabaloo* at the zoo.

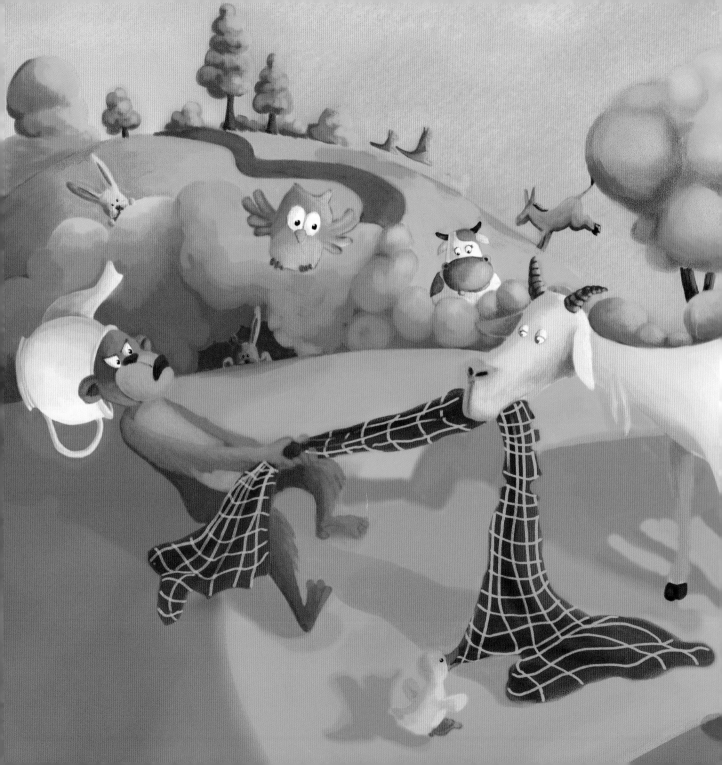

There's a hungry goat whose horns are all askew,
There are baby owls who sit and say "Twit-to-woo!"
Beside a roo called Sue with her joey, Blue,
who bounce around (that's all they do!)
And downy ducklings marching through!
Past a calf called Cassie who keeps on saying "Moo!"
And hopping bunnies with lots of grass to chew,
While the chimp twins, Daisy and Maisie, enjoy their tea-for-two,
With the cockatoo who squawks out "Boo!"
And a donkey called Drew

Making a *hullabaloo* at the zoo.

Don't forget Dapple the horse—
we must include him too!
There's a hungry goat whose horns are all askew,
There are baby owls who sit and say "Twit-to-woo!"
Beside a roo called Sue with her joey, Blue,
who bounce around (that's all they do!)
And downy ducklings marching through!
Past a calf called Cassie who keeps on saying "Moo!"
And hopping bunnies with lots of grass to chew,
While the chimp twins, Daisy and Maisie, enjoy their tea-for-two,
With the cockatoo who squawks out "Boo!"
And a donkey called Drew

Making a *hullabaloo* at the zoo.

There's someone missing from the **hullabaloo** at the zoo!

Who?